Andrew
and the Bee

Written by Rochelle Haynes

MOLO GLOBAL
PUBLISHING

ISBN Paperback: 978-1-7350720-4-3
ISBN E-book: 978-1-7350720-7-4
Library of Congress Control Number: 2020925523
© Rochelle Haynes, 2021 All Rights Reserved.

Published in Silver Spring, Maryland by Molo Global Publishing, an
imprint of Molo Global Consulting, LLC.

To my son:

I want you to believe deep in your heart
that you are capable of being anything you want to be,
and that you can achieve anything that you put your mind to!
Remember how much you are loved...
I am so immensely proud to have a son
like you Andrew Harris-Haynes II!

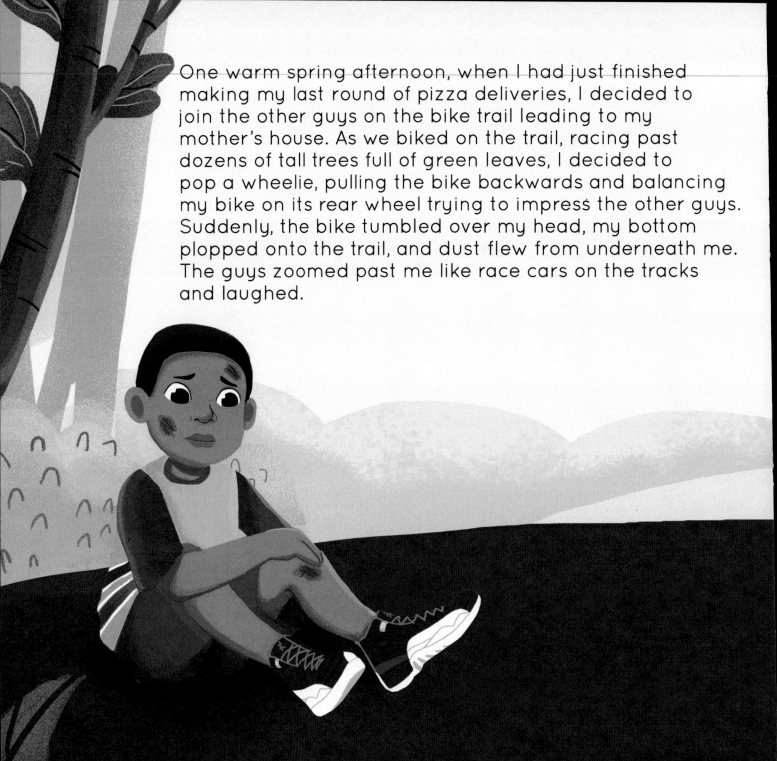

One warm spring afternoon, when I had just finished making my last round of pizza deliveries, I decided to join the other guys on the bike trail leading to my mother's house. As we biked on the trail, racing past dozens of tall trees full of green leaves, I decided to pop a wheelie, pulling the bike backwards and balancing my bike on its rear wheel trying to impress the other guys. Suddenly, the bike tumbled over my head, my bottom plopped onto the trail, and dust flew from underneath me. The guys zoomed past me like race cars on the tracks and laughed.

"Ouch!" I yelled, "that surely hurt."
I don't know how I'm going to tell my mother about how my handlebars got bent. She always told me
to be careful and not to perform any dangerous tricks on my bike, because I could get hurt.

Then something caught my eye.
There was a small sparkling thing that had flown
onto the top of my hand.

"That's what you get for showing off, you big dumbo!"
a squeaky little voice said.

I had to blink twice, I could not believe my eyes!
Sitting on my hand was the prettiest little bumble bee
that I had ever seen. It was yellow and black, and its
spots sparkled like silver glitter.
Was this who was talking to me?

I stared in disbelief, "What's
wrong with you, clumsy boy?
You've never seen a bumble bee
before?" asked the bumble bee.

"Yes, but not a sparkling bumble bee ...that talks."
The bumble bee extended her wings and zipped past
my ears, laughing while I stood still in shock.

"Tell me your name shorty," said the bumble bee.

I answered with stumbling words, "An, An, Andrew."

"Well Andrew, do you want me to fix those handlebars for you?" she asked. I glanced at the bumble bee and thought to myself, there is no way that this tiny little bumble bee could help me fix my handlebars.

"Hello?" said the bumble bee, waiting for me to respond.

"Um, okay sure," I replied. I stood up and began to pick up my bike.

"Follow me!" ordered the bumble bee.

I started to follow but quickly came to a stop;
"excuse me, but are you going to tell me your
name...and where are you leading me to?"
I asked.

"I knew you'd ask me that,"
said the bumble bee." "Well, my
name is Raquel, and I am taking
you to my palace," she replied.

"Your palace? What do you mean
by your palace?" I asked.

"I live in a palace because I am a princess," the bumble bee answered. I could not believe it, I was in awe. I began to chuckle, and I felt like I was dreaming.

"What's funny shorty?" asked the princess.

"Well if you're a princess, how did you become a bumble bee?" I asked.

As we continued on our journey, Raquel began to explain to me how she was turned into a bumble bee. "Well, my brother Tariq turned me into a bumble bee because he was upset with me. I would call him names and feed his dinner to my dog Kingston. I was always annoying him. Then one day when I was out on the balcony enjoying the nice cool breeze, my brother added a magic potion to my sweet lemon iced tea. He then brought it over to me suggesting that I take a sip and cool off. I felt a sense of suspicion because he hadn't done anything nice for me in a long time. He usually didn't pay me any attention, but I took it and sipped the tea, enjoying the lemon aroma as Tariq watched.

All a sudden, there was this bright shining light, and I began to shrink. My outfit fell to the ground and Tariq began to laugh.

"I got you now Raquel. This should teach you how to treat people," Tariq said with a wicked smile on his face.

We continued onto the terrain, then I realized that we were traveling through the beautiful green Congo rainforest located miles and miles away from my home! It was along the Atlantic Ocean on the west side of the African continent.

I could not believe how far we traveled!

As I continued listening to Raquel's story about why she was turned into a bumble bee, we passed by purple orchids, a family of elephants drinking water from a river, and I even saw a group of monkeys munching on monkey fruit. Raquel then paused and we came to a stop.

"I have a question Andrew," Raquel said, "after I fix your handlebars, will you help me to convince my brother that I do nice things, and that I can be nice to him and others?"

"I will certainly help you Princess Raquel," I answered. So we began walking once more towards the palace.

We soon arrived at Princess Raquel's palace, it was like my mother's house, but it was huge and surrounded by thousands of acres and wildlife. Raquel then led me into a part of the palace that looked like a mechanic's garage. She put my bike into this huge silver machine which had pulleys that tugged on my handlebars, and straightened them instantly.

"Here you are, just like new" said Raquel.

"Thanks, I don't know what I would've done without you." I hopped onto my bike and rode away never looking back. It was starting to get dark outside, and I knew that I had to be back home so that my mother wouldn't worry about me.

"Wait! Wait!" yelled Raquel.

She began to cry as Andrew rode
into the forest heading
towards his home. "Oh, what am
I to do now?" Raquel mumbled sadly.

The next day after I finished my pizza deliveries,
I entered the bike trail and went straight home.
I was so tired that I could barely keep my eyes open!
I propped my bike against the house and went inside.

Cling!

I heard a sound from the living room window,
but I was so exhausted that I ignored it
and plopped down onto the couch.

Cling!

I heard the sound again, so I sat up and looked
around. There, I saw something sparkling and
hovering in front of my living room window,
it was Raquel. I was quite surprised.

"How did she find me?" I thought to myself.
I leaped down the hallway like a cheetah
trying to catch its prey, and I hid in
my mother's closet.

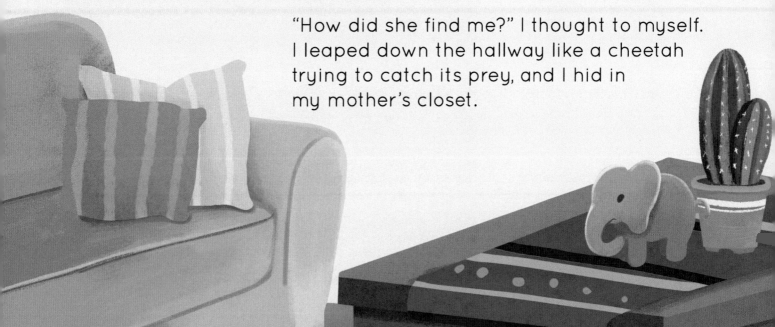

"Hey, come back here!" the bumble bee yelled.

"You promised you would help me if I fixed the handlebars on your bike!" the bumble bee said angrily.

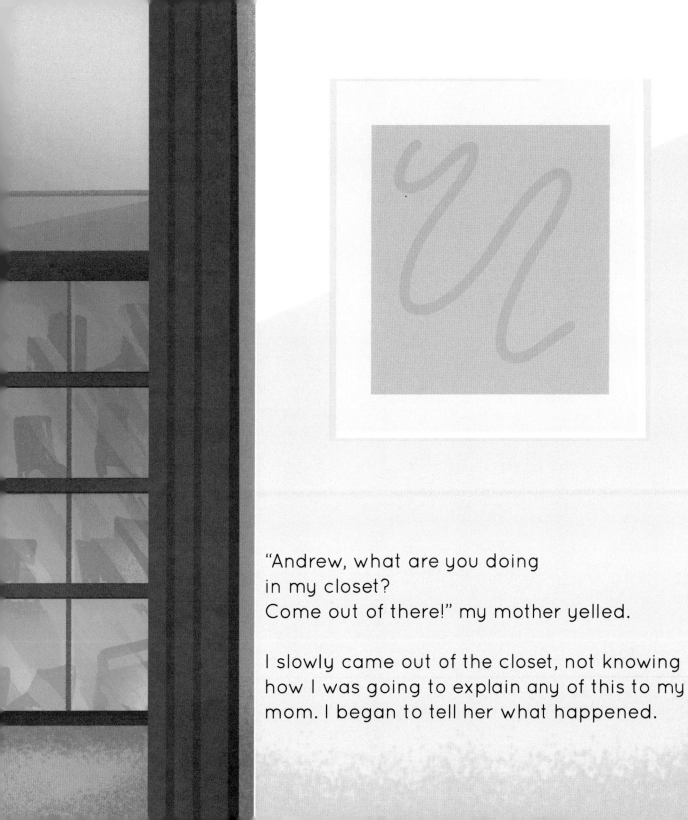

"Andrew, what are you doing
in my closet?
Come out of there!" my mother yelled.

I slowly came out of the closet, not knowing
how I was going to explain any of this to my
mom. I began to tell her what happened.

"Well mom, I was riding my bike on the trail after work yesterday, and thought it would be cool to show some of the guys that I could pop wheelies too... and then boom - my bike flipped over, and the handlebars got bent. I know that you told me not to do any dangerous tricks, but all the other guys were popping wheelies on the bike trail, so I wanted to show them that I could too.

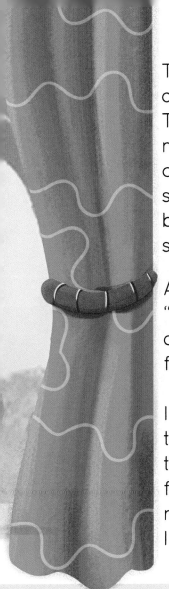

Then, this talking bumble bee appeared out of nowhere and assured me that she could help to fix my handlebars. That is not all though, she is also a princess. She made me promise to help her break the spell that her brother cast upon her, if she helped to fix my handlebars. So, she led me to her palace, and she fixed my bike. I broke my promise to her and rode off. Now she's outside of our window."

Andrew's mother stared, looking shocked, "Well Andrew, it is important to be honest and keep your word. So, now you must fulfill your promise."

I looked into my mother's eyes and said to her, "I know mom that's what you always told me. I will go and apologize to her, and fulfill my promise. Then, I walked out of my mother's bedroom and opened the living room window.

"Raquel, I am sorry that I didn't keep my promise. I will be right out to help you." I came outside still dressed in my uniform and got on my bike.

"Lead the way!" I told her. Raquel led me back through the forest to her palace. As we approached the palace, Raquel explained to me I could help her.

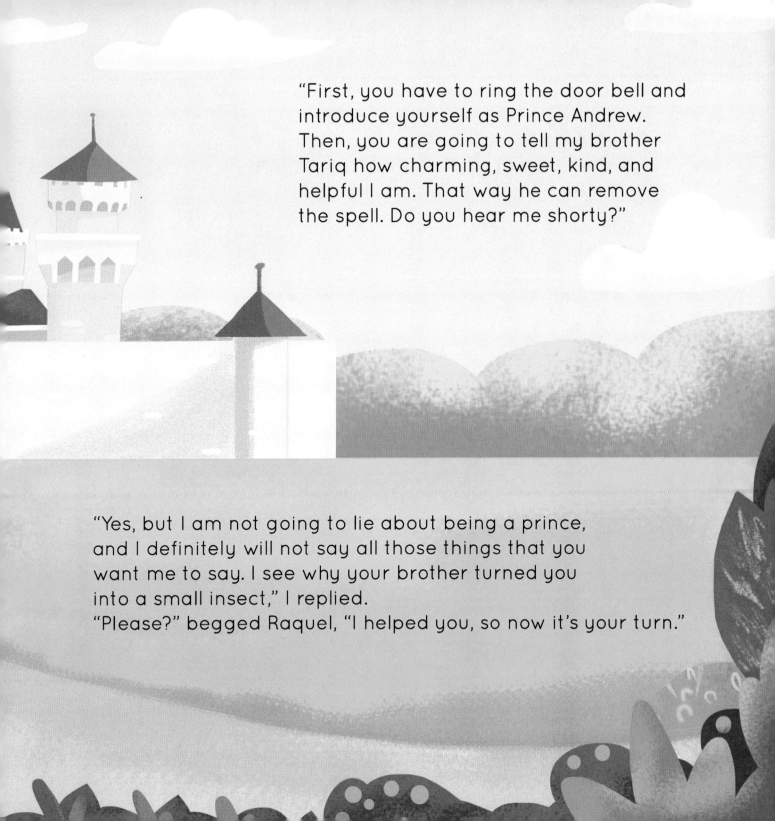

"First, you have to ring the door bell and introduce yourself as Prince Andrew. Then, you are going to tell my brother Tariq how charming, sweet, kind, and helpful I am. That way he can remove the spell. Do you hear me shorty?"

"Yes, but I am not going to lie about being a prince, and I definitely will not say all those things that you want me to say. I see why your brother turned you into a small insect," I replied.

"Please?" begged Raquel, "I helped you, so now it's your turn."

I then walked up to the big gate in front of the palace and rang the doorbell. A masculine loud voice spoke from the intercom.

"Who's there?" asked
Princess Raquel's brother.

"Prince Andrew sir," I responded
nervously. Raquel's brother Tariq
then invited me into the palace.

I walked in, and I was truly amazed at all the beautiful things that I saw inside.

"My, what a beautiful palace," I said to Tariq. I was amazed! I stood in the middle of the dining room looking around admiring all the golden framed artwork of jungle animals, and the golden vases accented with colored jewels. The dining table filled the room alongside chairs accented in shiny gold.

Tariq cleared his throat, "So, Prince Andrew how can I help you sir?"

"Oh, pardon me. I am here because I need to speak with you about Princess Raquel. I know that she may appear to be hard to get along with, but there is a good reason why she's been behaving in such a way," I explained.

"Is that so?" Tariq replied.

"Go on, I'm listening."

I then began to extend my hand and Princess Raquel flew over and landed on my palm. "Well, I will do Princess Raquel the honor and let her speak to you herself, as it will be more meaningful and heartfelt," I said to Tariq.

Tariq stared at her and said, "What is it Raquel?"

She continued to explain, "Andrew really isn't a prince, I asked him to pretend to be one so that you would let him enter into the palace and hear him out." Raquel stood timidly not knowing how Tariq would react.

"This is rather shocking," Tariq replied. "Andrew sir, you presented yourself in such a way that I couldn't tell the difference. I am still thankful for what you have done. In any case, we must find a way to repay you," said Tariq.

"Oh no sir, it was my pleasure. Princess Raquel has already given me something valuable, she fixed the handlebars on my favorite bike. It is the least I could do." I turned away and prepared to return home.

Princess Raquel ran towards Andrew and yelled, "Wait, I have something that I would like to say." I stopped walking and turned towards her. "Since you have come along on this journey with me, you have shown me that you are a trustworthy person; you helped me to do something that I thought I never would." Princess Raquel grabbed my hands firmly and looked into my eyes as I stared back into hers. "You make me feel safe when I am with you Andrew, and you make me smile more than I have in a long time.
Will you be my prince?" she asked.

I smiled and said with excitement, "I will, I will gladly become your prince!"

Princess Raquel was so excited, she yelled, "I've finally found my true love!"

Tariq ran through the palace yelling "my sister has found true love!" while everyone inside of the palace gathered around us.
Princess Raquel announced that she was so happy to find her prince!

They even went back to the bike trail where they met, and Raquel found someone each day and performed a good deed. Andrew grew to understand even more that Raquel was a good person and wonderful princess. Seeing her treat others with kindness made Andrew proud to be her prince.

When the wedding day arrived, Raquel chose to invite everyone that she and Andrew had helped to celebrate their marriage. As their family and friends gathered, they chanted well wishes to Princess Raquel and Prince Andrew.

They ate abundantly, and danced tirelessly into the night. Andrew was filled with joy while remembering his mother telling him that keeping promises and helping others would pay off in ways that he could never imagine.

ABOUT THE AUTHOR

Rochelle Haynes is a wonderful mother to a special young boy, a fiancée, and a small business owner. She runs Naturally Beautiful, a company that creates and sells handmade lip wear and other items. Rochelle loves children, and she loves spending time with her family and cute little yorkie Kingston. If she is not spending time with family, then she is working and thinking of more ways that she can make a better life for herself and her family. She completed an Early Childhood Education program at the Highland Springs VA Technical Center, earning her CDA. She then worked in childcare for a few years, and later graduated from the Medical Careers Institute with her Associate of Science Degree, as a Medical Assistant. From there, she gained her EMT-B licensure, and Nursing Assistant certification. Rochelle enjoys helping others when she is able to, and she has a very animated personality. Rochelle is now a first-time author of the fictional fairy tale, "Andrew and the Bee," and she plans to continue writing many more children's stories. She is such a busy bee!

Made in the USA
Middletown, DE
20 April 2022

64549457R10022